Billy Burger, Model Citizen is published by
Stone Arch Books,
A Capstone Imprint
1710 Roe Crest Drive
North Mankato, Minnesota 56003
www.mycapstone.com

Library of Congress Cataloging-in-Publication Data
The ferret fiasco / by John Sazaklis; illustrated by Lee Robinson.
     pages cm — (Billy Burger, model citizen)
  Summary: When third-grader Billy Burger takes the class pet ferret to the school assembly it
gets away, and Billy finds himself in trouble with the school and his detective father.
  ISBN 978-1-4965-2589-5 (library binding)
  ISBN 978-1-4965-2686-1 (paperback)
  ISBN 978-1-4965-2690-8 (ebook pdf)
1. Ferret—Juvenile fiction. 2. Elementary schools—Juvenile fiction. 3. Families—Juvenile
fiction. [1. Behavior—Fiction. 2. Conduct of life—Fiction. 3. Ferret—Fiction. 4. Schools—
Fiction.] I. Robinson, Lee (Illustrator), illustrator. II. Title.
  PZ7.S27587Fe 2016
  813.6—dc23
  [Fic]   2015025064

Illustrations by: Lee Robinson
Book design by: Ted Williams
Photo credit: Krithika Mahalingam Photography (mahalphoto.com), pg 94

Printed in the United States of America in Stevens Point, Wisconsin.
092015   009222WZS16

Billy Burger
MODEL CITIZEN

THE FERRET FIASCO

BY JOHN SAZAKLIS

STONE ARCH BOOKS
a capstone imprint

Table of Contents

HEY, WHAT'S UP?

MY NAME IS
BILLY BURGER.

Nice to meet you! If you're reading this, you have good taste in books. Now that I know something about you, how about I tell you something about me?

I live with my family in a medium-sized house, in a little town called Hicksville, in the big state of New York. Our medium-sized house got much smaller the same time my family got a little bigger—when my baby sister, Ruby, was born. She's kind of cute . . . if you like stinky, smelly, noisemakers!

My parents both work at the Hicksville Police Department. Pretty cool, huh? Dad is a detective. Mom is a criminal psychologist. Together, they solve mysteries and catch troublemakers. Now that I think about it, that isn't much different than taking care of me!

But I wouldn't call myself a troublemaker, exactly. I prefer the term *adventurer*. I'm always looking for interesting things to do or discover because I get bored easily. I think it's because I have an overactive imagination.

(Want to know what's more overactive than my imagination? My appetite! I love to eat, and sometimes I think about that more than anything else. Seriously. I'll try anything . . . twice!)

I usually don't go on adventures alone. My partner in crime is also my best friend, Teddy. He lives a few houses down from me on the same block. I'm always trying to think of fun things for us to do together!

When I get an idea it is usually awesomely epic. Unfortunately, my ideas don't always go as planned, and that's when I get in trouble.

But I'm working on that.

I'm working on being a better person, a better student, a better everything. Just like my grandpa, William Burger—the Hero of Hicksville. He's sort of a legend in our town. He did good deeds and inspired others to do the same.

And like Grandpa, I'm going to do just that.

I'm going to become **BILLY BURGER: MODEL CITIZEN!**

1
Morning Madness

BEEP, BEEP, BEEP!

The alarm clock screams in my ear.

"Ack!" I cry, sitting up in bed.

Why is that thing going off on a Saturday? I wonder. *Maybe I forgot to shut it off.*

I flip the switch so the alarm clock does not disturb me. Then I nestle back into my bed.

Drifting back to dreamland, I think to myself. *Saturday is the best day. You don't have to go to school on Saturday. Plus when you go to sleep at night, you don't have to wake up and go to school on Sunday! Isn't that great? If you ask me, there should be more Saturdays and Sundays in the week.*

My eyelids get heavier and finally close.

BAM! BAM! BAM!

"Ack!" I cry again.

This time I jump out of bed and open my door. My mom is standing there ready to knock on my head.

"Billy, wake up!" she says.

"I am awake," I reply.

Mom looks down at me and says, "Oh, I've been calling you for five minutes!"

"What for?" I ask.

"You're going to be late for school!" she replies.

I stare at her for a moment. "What? We don't have school on Saturday."

"It's Friday, Billy," my mom says.

"SAY WHAT?!" I say. I'm so confused. "What sorcery is this?"

"Friday has always come after Thursday as long as I've been alive," Mom replies.

"UGH," I groan.

Friday.

Not as great as Saturday, but it's better than Sunday. At least you don't have to go to school the next day.

"Okay, okay, let's get this over with," I say. I follow my mom into the kitchen. That's where Dad is.

He is whirling around like a tornado, making breakfast and packing our lunches before work. He's like a superhero!

Actually, he *is* a hero in real life.

My father is an undercover detective for the police department. Sometimes he gets to dress up and pretend to be someone else. Then he fools criminals by catching them in the act. Most of the time he investigates clues to solve mysteries. Isn't that cool?

"Breakfast is getting cold, Billy," he says. He scrapes scrambled eggs onto my plate.

"Good morning, sweetie," Mom says to Dad. "I love it when you make breakfast!"

She kisses him.

On the lips.

"EWW," I groan, covering my eyes. "I'm gonna lose my appetite. And that *never* happens."

Mom also works at the police department. That's how she and Dad met. She's a criminal psychologist. She studies why criminals do what they do. And she tries to help them change their ways to be better citizens.

Yeah, my parents are pretty awesome.

When they're not kissing, that is. **UGH!**

"I have a very big meeting today," Dad says to Mom while she eats her breakfast. He chugs the rest of his coffee and adds, "Your lunchbox is on the counter, Billy. Don't forget it."

Like I'd ever forget lunch. It's the second most important meal of the day.

Suddenly a high-pitched shriek fills the air. This one is even louder than my alarm clock.

WAAAAAAAAAAAAAAH!

"Ah," Mom says, calmly sipping her coffee. "Someone else wants her breakfast too."

That shrieking siren would be my baby sister, Ruby.

Mom works part-time so she can take care of Ruby during the day. Then Dad watches her at night when Mom is with patients.

"I'm coming, sweetheart," Mom says in her sweet singsong voice. My sister just screams louder.

If you ask me, babies don't have a lot of patience. They're always **SO** demanding.

I cover my ears to block out the screaming. But then I realize I can't eat my eggs without my hands. So I lean forward and start scooping up the eggs with my mouth.

"Quit that, Billy," Dad says. "You're not a dog."

"Woof!" I bark at him.

He rubs my head and holds out his fist. "You've got spunk, kid, I'll give you that."

I fist bump him back, and he kisses my head.

"DAAAD," I groan.

"What? I love you guys. You'll know what it's like someday," he says.

Mom comes back with my little sister. She's feeding her a bottle.

As soon as she sees me, Ruby pops the bottle out of her mouth and smiles. Her two little bottom teeth are pointing up. She's kind of cute when she's not screaming.

Or crying.

Or stinking up the place when she poops.

"AWW," Mom gushes.

Ruby reaches out and touches my face. Then she grabs my ear and pulls it.

"OW!"

Ruby laughs and claps her hands. Mom and Dad smile at her.

I roll my eyes, pick up my plate, and move to the other end of the table. "When I get married, I'm living alone," I say.

My parents laugh at my joke. Only they don't know I'm serious.

I finish my eggs along with the toast and drink my orange juice. Then I clean off my dishes and put them in the dishwasher.

"Thanks, buddy," Dad says. "Now go get dressed so you don't miss the bus."

"Oh, I don't mind missing the bus," I reply with a grin.

"Move it, mister!" Mom says, giving me her I-mean-business stare.

"Yes, ma'am." I salute and run away before she shoots laser beams out of her eyes and burns my butt. That's a super power *all* moms have, so be careful.

Once I'm in my room, the first thing I do is make my bed.

I know, I know. Who cares, right? You're just going to mess it up again. But Mom says it'll make me a better citizen. I do it for her. Plus, it's not so bad once you get used to it.

You wanna know bad?

Try doing fractions! We have a quiz at school today. I fried my brain last night going over practice problems with my dad.

That's probably why I woke up thinking it was Saturday. I guess I wished that Friday would disappear and take that awful math quiz with it!

Finally, I get dressed, grab my schoolbag, and meet Dad by the door. We bundle up because it's *so* cold out.

It hasn't snowed yet, but I keep praying for a blizzard. One so huge it buries the whole school. Twice.

Dad kisses Mom and my sister goodbye. I wave from afar so Ruby doesn't pull my ear again.

"Let's do this," Dad says, opening the door.

A cold blast of air hits us.

"Ready or not, here we go!"

2
Math Problems

We walk to the corner. My best friend, Teddy is waiting at the bus stop. He lives four houses down from me. I've known him my whole life. That's almost nine years! A long time, right?

"Hey, Billy," he says. "Happy Friday!"

"I'll be happy when it's Saturday," I reply.

We get on the bus, and most of the seats are taken. That's fine. We prefer to sit all the way in the back so we can look out the window and make faces at cars.

One time we made a face at a car . . . and it was my dad!

He didn't think it was funny.

And I got in trouble.

I know I'm not supposed to make faces at drivers anymore, but I can't help it. Sometimes, it just happens!

"Look at the Wonder Weirdos!" shouts Randy. He's this tall, angry-looking kid with long hair. His only interest is picking on smaller kids.

"Yeah," I answer him. "We're the Wonder Weirdos, because we *wonder* where *weirdos* like you come from!"

Teddy chimes in after me. "Under a rock maybe, like all the other slugs?"

Randy tries to come back with a better insult. He scrunches up his face like he's thinking really hard. It may even stay like that forever.

"Oh, yeah?" he shouts. "We'll you're—"

"Whaddya got, smart guy?" I shout, cutting him off. Dad says that bullies are usually just full of hot air. Sometimes you need to deflate them.

"Settle down back there!" yells the bus driver.

Teddy and I ignore Randy and find our seats.

"What are we going to do today, Billy?" Teddy asks.

"The same thing we do every day," I respond. "Try to take over the world!"

● ● ●

Soon we're pulling up to Fork Lane Elementary School. I like the name of our school. It makes me think of food.

I like food. Sometimes I eat too much food, and my mom tells me I need to slow down. But I think I'm just hitting a growth spurt . . . every day.

Even as I'm telling you this, I'm thinking about my lunch. Today I'm having a turkey and cheese sandwich. *Mmm.* Delicious!

There's a bag of baby carrots in there too. I like pretending I'm a huge giant and the carrots are little tiny people that I gobble up! Teddy's older brother says it's a babyish thing to do. But I still do it . . . just when no one is looking.

The bus empties out and Teddy and I walk down the west wing of the school to get to our third-grade class with Mr. Karas.

Mr. Karas has a beard and is really nice. Sometimes he brings his guitar to class and helps us learn things with songs. Some kids think he's geeky, but I think he's cool. He actually makes learning fun.

"Okay, class, first things first," he says. "Quiz time! Let's get the fractions out of the way while they're still fresh in your head."

Everybody groans.

"After the quiz, I'll tell you all about a special event that's happening today!"

As he hands out the papers, Mr. Karas stops by my desk. "Good morning, Billy," he says. "I hope you studied your fractions."

"I sure did," I say. "I propose we only take *half* the quiz!"

The class laughs.

"Very clever, Billy, but the answer is no," my teacher tells me.

"How about a *quarter* of the quiz?" I ask. "That's my final offer!"

The class laughs again.

But Mr. Karas writes my name on the board.

"First warning, Burger," he says. "Three strikes and you're out!"

3
Lunchtime...
Finally!

After I hand in my quiz, I slump down in my chair.
I tune out as Mr. Karas tells the class about today's
special event.

"We're having a guest speaker!" Mr. Karas says
cheerily. "He's going to talk to us about the new exhibit
at the Hicksville Museum of Natural History!"

The museum? **BORING**.

Some kids are excited since we were learning about
ancient artifacts. But I would have preferred the guest
speaker to be an escape artist like Harry Houdini.

Also, I'm upset that school has barely started and my
name is already on the board.

Three strikes is a trip to the principal's office, and I already have one. I'm bound to mess up once after lunch. So for the rest of the morning, I have to behave.

I for sure have to keep my comments on the museum and Harry Houdini to myself.

• • •

As soon as Mr. Karas says it's lunchtime, I shoot out of my chair like a rocket and head straight to my cubby in the back of the room.

Teddy zooms up next to me. Together we stop by Franklin's cage.

Franklin the ferret is our class pet. He's named after Benjamin Franklin. Old Ben is one of our Founding Fathers. He's also the dude who discovered that lightning is made up of electricity. (I think that's a pretty *shocking* discovery, don't you?)

"Hey, Franklin," I say. "How's it going?" I poke my finger into the cage

Franklin scurries across the wood shavings and sniffs my finger. I sneak him a snack from the pet food box when nobody's looking. "Have a good lunch, little buddy," I say.

Then Teddy and I get in line and head out to the cafeteria.

We always sit with our friends Mike and Jason for lunch. I trade Jason some of my carrots for his potato chips. Some. But not all. That way I can say that I ate my veggies at lunch if anyone asks.

We dig into our food and chomp away like it's feeding time at the zoo.

Mike breaks the silence. "So, what did you think of yesterday's episode?" he asks.

"Oh, man! It was so **AWESOME!**" I reply.

"It was so **EPIC**," Jason says

"It was so **AWESOMELY EPIC!**" Teddy exclaims.

"Okay, you win, Teddy," we say.

We are talking about one of our favorite cartoons, *Super Samurai from Outer Space.*

The show is about four Samurai brothers from ancient Japan. They found a meteorite that had crash-landed in their village. When they touched it, they were transformed into super warrior astronauts.

Now they have the power to travel through the galaxy at the speed of light. Their new mission is to fight aliens and monsters who are trying to destroy the universe.

In last night's show, a tyrant named Lord Pyros wanted to gain control of a magic crystal. It belonged to a powerful sorceress. The crystal could grant unbelievable power to the person who possessed it.

With it, Lord Pyros would be able to control every planet in the solar system. It was up to the Super Samurai to join forces with the sorceress to stop him.

After an awesomely epic battle, the episode ended with the tyrant getting his hands on the crystal. He was about to unleash its power!

"Can you believe it's **TO BE CONTINUED?**" I say.

"I hate when they do that!" Jason replies.

"My brother says that it's going to be a four-part story," Teddy tells us.

"Four parts!" I exclaim. **"SAY WHAT?!"**

"How does he know?" Mike asks.

"Well," Teddy says, "it's based on the original comic book series. *That* story line was four issues long. So they're probably going to break up the TV show into four episodes. Each one based on a different issue."

"Whoa," I say. "Cool."

"*Then*," Teddy adds, "my brother says that the sorceress gets possessed by an evil spirit. And the Samurai have to fight—"

"Spoiler alert!" Mike shouts. He covers Teddy's mouth. "Don't ruin it for the rest of us!"

"Yeah!" Jason and I say.

"Sorry, guys," Teddy replies.

"It's okay," I tell him. "I'll try to forget it by the end of the day. I'm sure that assembly will put us to sleep, anyway."

The guys laugh at my joke. We all make loud snoring sounds.

The lunch monitor walks by. "A little less noise, please," she says. "You sound like hungry pigs on a farm."

"That's because we are," I whisper. "Oink, oink!"

We cover our mouths and snicker to each other.

● ● ●

After lunch and recess, I sit at my desk and wonder what to do with myself. Mr. Karas said the assembly was going to be an hour long.

A **WHOLE** hour.

Sixty minutes.

Listening to a guy talk about boring museum stuff.

I dig around inside my desk for anything to keep me busy. A broken puzzle, a rubber band ball, a couple of baseball cards.

Nothing.

What could I possibly bring to the assembly that will keep me entertained? I mean, I could try to pay attention, but . . .

Suddenly something moves behind me. I turn to see Franklin shifting in his cage. He is stretching his arms and yawning.

A lightbulb goes off inside my head.

"BINGO!" I say.

4
Mission Accomplished

How am I going to pull this off? I wonder. *This is why superheroes have sidekicks.*

If Teddy and I were a dynamic duo, he would totally be my sidekick.

I lean over toward Teddy's desk.

"*Psst.* I need you to do me a solid," I whisper.

"A solid? What do you mean? Like solids, liquids, and gases? We're not doing science right now," he whispers back.

"That's not what I mean. I need you to do me a favor," I explain.

Teddy nods. "Oh, right. Sure. What is it?"

"I need you to distract Mr. Karas while I get Franklin out of his cage."

"Why?" my friend asks.

"So we can bring him to the assembly with us. Duh!" I whisper loudly.

"**AW, YEAH!** Great idea!" Teddy says.

"I know, right? I truly *am* a genius!" I say and lean back in my seat.

"Hey, what are you guys whispering about?" asks Parker. He's stretched his entire body across the aisle to stick his big nose in our business.

What a snoop! He probably wants to know everything and then tattle on us for no good reason. That's what he usually does.

"None of your beeswax," I hiss.

"Did you say something about the ferret?" he asks.

"This is an A and B conversation," I say. I point to Teddy and myself. "So C yourself out of it!"

Parker huffs and returns to his upright position.

"Okay . . . um . . ." Teddy taps his head while he thinks and says, "**AHA!** I've got it. Watch the master at work."

He cracks his knuckles and gets out of his seat.

My best friend walks up to Mr. Karas's desk. I wait a
few seconds until Teddy is blocking his view. Then I rush
over to the cage.

I quietly open the door and put my hand inside. I
wait for Franklin to get used to my smell. He really likes
to play if he recognizes you.

One time, Sally tried to grab him too quickly and
Franklin attacked. He didn't bite her, but he sprayed her
with his butt juice.

Ferrets are like skunks. They spray an awful odor
when they feel threatened.

Sally stank for two days. No one could even sit next to her. And she had to use a special soap from the doctor until the smell went away.

But thanks to her, we all learned a valuable lesson.

Franklin fidgets and grunts. Then he crawls over to lick my fingers. I grab a few of his snacks, pop them into my pocket, and quickly scoop him up. I hold him tight so he doesn't scurry.

CLANG! The metal door slams shut.

Mr. Karas asks, "What was that?"

I shove Franklin under my sweatshirt and slide into my seat faster than a ninja.

Fortunately, the principal's voice comes over the PA system. Mr. Karas forgets about the clang.

"Good afternoon, students and faculty. This is Principal Crank. Please begin to prepare for this afternoon's assembly in the auditorium. We will begin promptly. Please do not delay. Thank you."

Mr. Karas asks us to get in line and stand by the door. Teddy and I stay at the end of the line, so he can't see us.

"I can't believe our plan worked," I whisper to Teddy.

As we walk to the auditorium, I can feel Franklin shifting under my shirt. We wait a few paces so that the rest of the class turns the corner. Then I lift my shirt up a bit so Franklin can peek his head out. The ferret sniffs the air around him. His whiskers twitch, and they tickle against me.

"Here, I brought some snacks," I say, handing them to Teddy. "Wanna feed him one?"

"Sure."

I hold Franklin's body while Teddy feeds him. The ferret uses his paws to nibble on the little treat. He really is cute.

"Maybe we can teach him a few tricks," Teddy says.

"Yeah," I reply. "Like how to spray on command whenever we see Randy on the bus."

"Ha-ha, yeah, like a super soaker." Teddy laughs.

"POINT, AIM, FIRE!"

Franklin finishes his treat and eyes the handful of snacks in Teddy's hand. He catches me off guard and tries to leap toward my friend.

Startled, Teddy yelps and drops the snacks. Franklin gets super hyper and struggles against me. His back paws scratch my stomach, and I lose my grip!

"OUCH!" I yelp. Franklin wiggles out of my hands!

He lands lightly and takes in his surroundings. Before Teddy and I can make a move, the ferret scurries down the hall!

"Oh, no!" Teddy cries. "We gotta get that class pet!"

"And fast!" I add.

5
Catch That Critter!

AUDITORIUM

Teddy and I chase after Franklin. The ferret senses
us behind him and scurries even faster. Luckily, everyone
else is already in the auditorium, so the main hallway is
completely empty.

"Catch that critter!" I yell in my very best Super
Samurai voice.

"Split up so we can corner him," Teddy replies.

When I zig toward Franklin, he zags toward Teddy.
When Teddy zags toward Franklin, he zigs toward me.

The fast little ferret runs right through my legs. I
bend over to watch him go.

"HA!" I laugh. "Ferrets look really funny from upside down."

"*You* look from funny upside down," Teddy says. "Now, let's go!"

This time Teddy zigs, while Franklin zags. And then I zag, and Franklin zigs!

"Oof," I say, leaning against the water fountain. "I need a drink."

"There's no time for that!" Teddy scolds. "Super Samurai don't stop for drinks."

"How do you know?" I ask.

"There are no water fountains in outer space," Teddy replies. **"DUH!"**

"Oh yeah, you have a point."

"Hey, I got an idea," Teddy shouts. He holds up the snacks.

"Snacks!" I shout. "Brilliant, Super Samurai Teddy!" I shout.

"Why thank you, Super Samurai Billy!" Teddy says.

Teddy takes a bow and chucks a few of the snacks at Franklin. The pet stops, sniffs the air, and starts to crawl slowly toward the ferret food. Teddy and I begin to creep slowly toward him.

It takes all of my Super Samurai stealth not to distract Franklin while he nibbles away at the treats. I'm almost on top of him when Teddy screams.

"GOTCHA!"

He pounces on Franklin and grabs him by his side. Teddy is not as stealthy as I am, but he's still effective. (Like I said—he's a sidekick and he's got a lot to learn.)

Franklin wriggles in my friend's grasp and manages to squeeze himself free. He bounds away from Teddy, right toward me.

He won't pass through my legs this time!

I buckle my knees and drop low, falling into a squat. I'm practically sitting on Franklin. He wriggles under my weight.

"I've got you now!" I yell.

"You'll crush him, Billy!" Teddy cries.

I glare at Teddy. "Just what are you trying to say?"

"Well, you did have **TWO** treats at lunch today." He pokes my stomach.

"Quit it!" I snap. "Help me get the pet before he bites my butt, will ya?"

"How?" Teddy asks.

"Reach under and grab him tight this time."

"EW," Teddy says, scrunching up his nose. "What if you fart in my face?"

"I'm not gonna fart in your face!" I shout. "If I did, it would knock your teeth out!"

"GROSS!" Teddy says, laughing. "Although, that *is* a lot of tooth fairy money."

"You're right. And I get fifty percent of that, which is *half* according to our fractions quiz!"

Suddenly, something moves underneath my rear.

"OUCH!" I yelp, jumping up. A sharp pain shoots through my right butt cheek. "He bit me!"

I hop up and down, rubbing my butt. It's a good thing no one is around to see this. I'd be the laughingstock of the school.

Franklin runs for it, but this time Teddy scoops him up and holds him close. "Got him!"

But then I start to panic. "What if there's venom pumping through my veins right now?"

"Ferrets don't have venom," Teddy says calmly.

"What about rabies?" I ask.

"Would he be in our class if he had rabies?" he points out.

"I don't know! What if I turn into a mutant ferret man?" I exclaim.

Teddy rolls his eyes. "**YEESH**, I thought *I* was the drama king," he says. "But you have to admit . . . it would be kind of awesome to become a mutant ferret man."

"You want him to bite you too?" I ask.

"No, thanks," Teddy says.

My friend holds the ferret away from him.

Franklin fidgets a little and then calms down.

I wipe the sweat from my forehead. "Let's see if we can sneak into that assembly without anyone noticing," I say.

Teddy and I peek through the window in the auditorium door.

"Yikes! It's Principal Crank," I whisper. "If he spots us, we're doomed. What's Plan B?"

"B? *Hmm*. B for backstage!" Teddy says. "Follow me."

Teddy knows his way around the auditorium. He played the title role in the school production of *Peter Pan* last year.

Teddy's a really good actor and singer and dancer. He'll probably be famous someday. By then, he'll need a bodyguard. That's where I come in. I'm gonna be his hired muscle. Just as soon as my childhood chub turns into my manly muscles.

We turn right, walking away from the entrance of the auditorium. Teddy leads me down the front hallway straight toward the main office.

"Wait! We can't pass the office," I remind him. "What if the secretary sees us? We'll get in trouble for sure."

"She won't see us," Teddy assures me. "Watch."

He crouches down and duckwalks under the secretary's window. My bottom is still sore, but I suck up the pain and follow my friend.

"Why do I let you drag me into these things?" I complain through gritted teeth.

"It was *your* idea, remember?" says Teddy.

"Oh, yeah. Never mind."

Once we pass the office, we straighten up and head toward the back end of the auditorium where there is a big, heavy door that leads backstage.

"Here, hold him," Teddy says. He hands me the naughty ferret.

Franklin sniffs my hands, realizes they are familiar, and crawls into my palms.

"I've got my eye on you, ferret!" I say to Franklin. "No more biting, or I'll bite you back!"

I could have sworn Franklin stuck his tongue out at me.

Teddy opens the big, heavy door and leads us backstage. Inside, there are trunks of clothes and piles of wooden props.

Some of the painted backdrops are hanging from metal rods behind the main stage.

"Oh, look, there's Skull Rock from Never Land," Teddy says.

That was my favorite part of the play—the part where Peter Pan fights Captain Hook to save Princess Tiger Lily.

Teddy reenacts a few fight moves, stabbing his imaginary sword into the air against an imaginary pirate.

Teddy has a vivid imagination, just like me. That's why we're best friends.

"I can't wait until they teach us *actual* stage combat in high school drama class," Teddy says.

"You can take a class just to learn to fight?" I ask.

"Yeah. Well, it's fake fighting so that no one gets hurt. But it still looks real," Teddy explains.

"That's cool," I say.

We pass the props and scenery and stand near the side of the stage where no one can see us. I catch a glimpse of the speaker onstage. He is wearing what looks like safari gear, with a really neat vest that has a hundred pockets on it.

Behind him is a table set up with a bunch of tools and supplies. There's a long, lumpy thing covered by a sheet. I wonder what it can be.

With the speaker is another man and two women. They are wearing similar outfits.

"My name is Minnesota Clark," says the man. "And I am lead archaeologist for the Hicksville Museum of Natural History. Behind me is my expedition team. And together," he says, pausing for dramatic effect, "we are treasure hunters!"

The crowd reacts excitedly.

Teddy and I stare at each other.

Even Franklin looks amazed.

"SAY WHAT?!"

6
Fast and Furious

"**NOW** we're talking!" Teddy says.

"Yeah! I didn't think a guest speaker could be this cool," I say. "I wish Mr. Karas had mentioned that. Then I wouldn't have chased the class pet around the hall and got bitten on the butt!"

Teddy laughs.

"Finding buried treasure takes a long time. It is a detailed process," Mr. Clark says. "We use a number of terrific tools to help us in our search."

He unrolls a long belt across the table and begins to describe its contents.

I zone out and focus on the mystery object under the sheet. Franklin shifts in my grip because he is getting restless.

"I don't blame you, buddy," I tell him.

"What do you think is under there?" Teddy asks.

I shrug.

"Come on, man," I urge the speaker. "Get to the good stuff!"

A picture appears on the screen behind them.

"Does anyone know what this is?" Mr. Clark asks.

"A Samurai!" shout a number of kids in the audience.

"Correct!" Mr. Clark continues. "Samurai were the warriors of ancient Japan!"

The crowd gasps as Minnesota Clark pulls away the sheet. There sits an original set of Samurai armor and a sword. It is the **COOLEST** thing I have ever seen.

Teddy and I are so distracted that we aren't paying attention to Franklin. He must still be hungry, because he starts nibbling away at the curtain rope hanging next to us.

By the time I realize what is going on and pull Franklin away, it's already too late. The crafty little critter has gnawed his way through the rope.

Suddenly it snaps. **WHOOSH!**

The heavy red curtain completely breaks loose. It comes crashing down on top of Minnesota Clark and his expedition team like a big blanket. **CRASH!**

"Oops," I squeak. Looks like the archaeologists are gonna need someone to dig *them* out!

Within seconds, there is chaos in the auditorium. People are shouting. Some of the kids are laughing. Others are crying.

Principal Crank is hollering at the top of his lungs as Mr. Karas and other teachers come running onto the stage.

We watch a jumble of arms and legs flailing about inside the curtain.

"We need to get out of here, fast!" I say.

"You're right!" says Teddy. "Follow me!"

My friend disappears behind the stage.

I move to follow him, but Franklin has another idea—he breaks free again!

Next time I take him out, I'm putting him on a leash!

I rush after the ferret as he runs across the stage. This time, I catch him right away.

"You've been caught!" I yell from the middle of the stage.

"You most certainly have!" booms a deep voice.

I turn to see Principal Crank standing over me. His steely gaze burns two holes into my soul. A shiver creeps up and down my spine.

I gulp and begin to sweat. *Something is pretty warm up here*, I say to myself. I turn toward the heat and realize that a blinding, white spotlight is pointed right at me.

GULP!

The entire auditorium falls silent. Mr. Karas and the other teachers help Minnesota Clark and his team to their feet.

I am currently the center of attention.

Beads of sweat trickle down my forehead. My heart is pounding and my knees are knocking together.

Far on the opposite side of the auditorium, I see Teddy standing at the top of the stairs. At least one of us managed to escape.

"Billy Burger!" shouts Principal Crank. "My office.

NOW!"

I glance at Mr. Karas. He looks really upset.

I follow the principal off the stage, and he stops me in my tracks. "Kindly return that rodent to your teacher," he commands.

I do as he says.

"George, I trust you to restore order here in my absence," he instructs Mr. Karas.

"Yes, sir," he replies. He takes Franklin from me. I can tell he is disappointed in me. He also seems to be afraid of the principal.

"Step lively, Mr. Burger. We have *much* to discuss," Principal Crank says, clapping his hands together.

I hang my head and march off to my doom.

7
Temple of Doom

I follow Principal Crank back to his office. It is the longest walk of my life. The hallways are completely quiet. All I can hear is the clack-clack-clack of the principal's super shiny shoes against the floor tile.

I stare at the shoes. Back and forth they go, shiny and black. I can see my face in them!

I wonder how long it takes him to polish them. Does he use spit? I doubt it. He probably has a fancy shoe polish that is only for principals. It probably costs thousands of dollars.

Once we are inside his office, Principal Crank shuts the door behind us. He sits at his desk, rubs his eyes, and lets out a deep sigh. I wonder why he always does that when I'm in here. Must be an adult thing.

"Where shall I even begin, Billy?" he asks. "That stunt you just pulled could have severely hurt someone! What was your reason for such behavior? Why were you lurking behind the stage? How did you get that rodent in your possession?"

I look down at my sneakers, unable to look him in the eye. My face is still burning as if a hundred spotlights are on me.

"Do you have anything to say for yourself?" he asks.

My mouth is dry and my throat is scratchy.

I actually don't have a good reason for my behavior, but I'm certainly not going to tell *him* that. I just wanted to have a little fun.

"Technically, Principal Crank," I say. "Ferrets are not rodents. We learned that in class."

"Do not make jokes!" he snaps. "This is a serious offense, Mr. Burger."

What kind of joke is that? I wonder to myself. *It doesn't even have a punch line.* Principal Crank probably doesn't know what a real joke sounds like. It might be because he doesn't have a sense of humor.

I decide the best thing to do is to keep my mouth shut, as hard as it is to do.

"You leave me no choice but to call your parents. I'm sure your father will not be pleased when he hears about this," says Principal Crank.

I want to yell, *There's no need to tell him!* But it is too late. The phone is already off the hook.

I wonder if he has my phone number on speed dial.

After a few rings, the other line picks up. Principal Crank tells my father everything that happened.

I hear my dad's voice on the other line. He does *not* sound happy.

Mr. Crank hangs up, and I just sit there, swinging my legs under the chair.

I look around the room. Everything is dreary and gray. The walls. The pictures on them. Even Principal Crank in his gray suit with his gray hair.

There is a knock at the door, and Mr. Karas enters.

"I'm here to report an update on the auditorium," he says. "The janitor rolled up the curtain and will have a crew repair it over the weekend. Minnesota Clark and his team are fine. They are continuing with their presentation. They said it was the most excitement they've had in a while. I guess that means they won't be suing the school, right?" My teacher lets out a nervous chuckle and stops short.

Principal Crank's face turns bright red like a strawberry. I can imagine steam shooting out of his ears.

"Do **NOT** make jokes!" he shouts.

Mr. Karas takes a step back.

I feel a little less alone. I guess grown-ups can get yelled at too.

"Well, if you'll excuse me, I'll return to the auditorium with the rest of my class. Billy, I hope this is a lesson to you," my teacher adds.

Mr. Karas walks out of the room, leaving me alone with Principal Crank again.

After waiting for what feels like five hundred forevers, my dad shows up. He nods at the principal and then looks down at me.

"On your feet, William," he says.

I get up and follow him out the door. For the second time that day, I march to my doom.

• • •

"What's going on here?" my mother asks in surprise as we walk in the door. She is hurriedly putting on her coat and shoes. Mom takes a look at Dad's face and knows that I'm in trouble.

They have this weird thing they do where they read each other's minds. It's so spooky.

I begin to plead my case, and my mother puts her finger to her lips.

"*Shhh*, I just put the baby to sleep. Grandma's here to help while I'm gone."

"I'll take care of this," my dad says. "You get to work so you're not late." They kiss each other goodbye, and my mom rushes out the door.

I unload my school stuff and kick my schoolbag across the floor. It skids to a stop right in front of another pair of legs.

"Good afternoon, William," says my grandmother.

"Good afternoon, Grandma," I reply.

Grandma says it's proper to address someone formally when you greet them. So that's what I do when only she's around.

Could you imagine me saying "good afternoon" to Teddy? We would probably have to wear top hats and tuxedos like those old-timey people in black and white movies.

Grandma walks over to me and gives me a kiss on both cheeks. Then she kisses my dad.

"You run off, dear," she says to my father. "I'll watch over the children."

Dad thanks her and turns to me.

"You and I are going to have a nice, long chat about your behavior at school as soon as I get back tonight," he says. "Enjoy your freedom while it lasts."

Before I can object, my father is out the door and gone.

Model Citizen

"Pay no attention to him," Grandma says. "Trust me. I know my son. When your father gets upset, his bark is usually worse than his bite."

BITE?

I think of what Franklin did to my butt and rub my cheek. Yep, it's still sore.

My grandmother sits down on the couch. She pats the seat next to her. I join her and give her a big hug. She smells like flowers and mothballs, but I like it.

"Do you remember your grandfather, William?"

I nod my head yes.

My grandfather was the *first* William Burger. He died last year around the time Ruby was born. I'm named after him, in case you hadn't guessed.

"William, your grandfather was a wonderful man. He was a loving husband and father. And he was a real war hero. In short, your grandfather was a model citizen," says Grandma. "When he came back from overseas, he continued to fight for his country by giving back to the community. Why do you think he has that monument in the Hicksville town square?"

Right across the library and near the train station is a large fountain dedicated to Grandpa. It's the William Burger Reflecting Pool. Says so right on a marble plaque at the base.

"Because he was a model citizen?" I guess.

"Exactly, my sweet child," she says.

I nod, picturing the fountain. We visit it all the time. Sometimes, Teddy and I throw coins in it to make our wishes come true. So far, I can't fly and Teddy doesn't have a dragon, but we're not giving up yet!

Grandma continues. "Your grandfather worked to feed the hungry. He helped the homeless get shelter. And he made sure the neighborhood was a good place for children. He did this all *on top* of providing for his family."

I stare at my shoes again.

"My darling, I'm not telling you all this to make you feel bad or sad. Heavens, no! I'm reminding you that you carry not only your grandfather's name, but everything it stands for. You must honor it as best as you can."

My body tingled. I felt like I was listening to the Super Samurai Grand Master give his speech about how great power comes with great responsibility.

"You're right, Grandma. I'm sorry about getting in trouble," I say.

I give her another hug. Then I sit quietly.

I wonder what it means to be a model citizen. I know that I need to stay out of trouble. But that's not all.

I know I have to do good things too. I should do things to help people like my grandpa did. I should help others just like Mom and Dad. Just like the Super Samurai!

"Darling, you have a rambunctious spirit like your grandfather," Grandma says.

She rubs my head. "He, too, was always getting in and out of mischief. One time your grandfather shaved off his general's mustache while the man was sleeping and glued it to his own face. Then he said to the general, 'I mustache you a question'!"

Grandma starts laughing at the memory.

I couldn't believe my ears. My grandpa did that? That's epically awesome!

"Did he get in trouble?" I ask.

"Of course he did," Grandma replies. "That is one way of learning from our mistakes. But let's see if we can use *your* powers for good . . . not evil! Ha-ha-ha-ha!"

"Grandma!" I say, surprised. "You sound just like my favorite cartoon."

"Do I?" she says with a wink.

Grandma leans forward and gives me a kiss on the head. Then she whispers, "I sure hope Lord Pyros doesn't get his hands on the magic crystal."

"SAY WHAT?!" I yell.

"Keep your voice down. You'll wake the baby!" Grandma says. "Now go get your books. We have homework to do. A sharp mind equals a strong body!"

• • •

Later that night, I help Grandma make dinner. Mom is working late tonight, and Ruby is playing in her playpen.

We are making Grandma's famous beef stew. My mouth is watering at the thought. I snack on some of the carrots and celery while we wait.

Grandma waves her finger at me. "Save some of those for the stew!"

"Yes, ma'am," I say, swallowing the last chunk of carrot.

Once the ingredients are all boiling in a pot, I hear the front door unlock.

My stomach does a flip.

I completely forgot that Dad and I were going to have a "talk" about my behavior. That usually means a punishment.

"If Dad asks, I got called away by the secret service to meet with the president!" I tell Grandma. Then I rush out of the kitchen looking for a place to hide.

I run straight for the living room and leap into the air. I slide headfirst across the living room carpet. I'm halfway underneath the sofa when my stomach gets stuck.

WHUMP!

"This is what I get for eating a snack before dinner." I grunt. My legs wriggle behind me as I try to squeeze the rest of my body under.

"FREEZE!" my father yells from the hallway. "Come out from under there this instant."

I push myself backward, but the sofa comes with me. I start to panic. What if I have to live the rest of my life like the Hunchback of Notre Dame? Only instead of a hump, I'll have a couch stuck to my back.

It's dark and hot, and I'm starting to sweat. "A little help, please?" I say.

Suddenly the sofa lifts off of me. I roll over onto my back. My dad is holding the couch up with one hand and offering me help with his other. I take ahold of it, and he hoists me onto my feet.

"Smooth," he says with a smirk.

Huffing and puffing, I fall on the couch.

"Make it quick!" I say dramatically. "Please don't make me suffer!"

"Well, you and I both know I'll have to punish you, Billy," Dad says. "But we've been through this before. Punishments don't always stick. I was your age once too. I know you have a huge amount of energy and creativity. Your mom and I have talked about putting you in after-school activities. It's just that money's a little tight right now."

He looks down at his hands and gets quiet.

"If I may," Grandma interrupts. "William and I were discussing the great deeds of his grandfather. Perhaps we should look to him for inspiration. *Hmm?*"

"What do you mean, Ma?" Dad asks.

"Well, I'll leave that to you . . . the world's greatest detective," she says.

Grandma fetches her purse and pulls out a folded-up newspaper. "Here is my copy of the *Hicksville Illustrated*," she says. "There are always volunteer events going on at the community center or at the church or even right here in your neighborhood."

Dad looks at the paper and rubs his chin. "*Hmm*, that's not a bad idea."

"You can always go *on the line* and find things," Grandma adds. "Or so I'm told."

"You mean *online*, Ma," Dad tells her. "That's what they call using the Internet."

"Quite right, dear," she replies, waving her arm. "Either way, it's a start."

Grandma goes back into the kitchen to finish her stew.

"Your grandma's pretty brilliant, isn't she?" Dad says with a smile.

He scans the paper quickly and frowns. "*Hmm*. I don't see anything here that's suitable for you, though."

I get a second wind and hop off the couch. "Hey, if you don't find anything, no biggie. The important thing is we tried, right? If you need me, I'll be playing *Super Samurai from Outer Space* on my GameBox."

"You most certainly will *not*," Dad scolds. "That GameBox is off limits until I say so."

"When will *that* be?" I whine.

"When I say so!" Dad says.

"**ARGH**," I cry, falling onto the couch.

"First thing in the morning, we're going to find you a nice volunteer activity. You are going to put your time and energy to good use."

On a Saturday? I think. ***DOUBLE ARGH!***

9

Snow Daze

The next morning, I dread getting out of bed. I'm sure whatever punishment awaits me will be terrible.

Then I remember what Grandma said. I shouldn't think of this as a punishment. I should think of this as an opportunity—a way to help my community.

Maybe I can even be a hero.

Would the Space Samurai shy away from a challenge? Never.

Then neither will I.

I will become Billy Burger, Model Citizen!

Leaping out of bed, I whirl the sheet over me and wrap it around my neck. "Billy Burger to the rescue!"

I jump over a pile of comic books.

"I'm not afraid of you, world," I yell as I pull my curtains open. "Give me your best shot!"

Suddenly I freeze in my tracks. **"SAY WHAT?!"**

I blink once.

Then once again.

Then twice more for good measure.

I rub my eyes to make sure I'm awake, and I even pinch myself to double check.

Looking out of the window, I see the most wonderful thing in the world—snow! Snow so thick that it covers our car's tires. It's a big, smooth, white blanket of spectacular snow covering everything in sight.

"HUZZAH!" I cheer. "My punishment has been blindsided by bad weather. Time for me to call Teddy so we can build a snow Samurai!"

"Not so fast, wise guy!" my dad calls out from the door. "I'm sure we'll find something for you to do down at the public library . . . just as soon as I dig the car out."

"Wha—?" I manage to say.

I do **NOT** want to be stuck inside some dusty old library. There's got to be something I can do that will keep me outside.

Suddenly, a lightbulb goes off. Dad's comment about digging out the car gives me an idea.

"Hey, Dad, I can help you shovel out the walkway and the driveway and the car," I say. "That's doing a good deed, right?"

"Well, you'd be helping me out. But I'm your father, so that doesn't really count," he says with a smile.

"Okay, fine, I'll even shovel Old Man Withers' driveway too. He's a nice guy," I add.

Dad rubs his chin and looks like he's forming a plan.

"That's not a bad idea, Billy," he says. "After you and I help shovel Old Man Withers' sidewalk and driveway, we are going to continue on shoveling until we help every elderly person on this block who can't do it on their own."

"This . . . this block?!" I stammer.

Me and my big mouth!

I rush to the window and start counting the houses. One, two, three, four . . . a **ZILLION**! I fling myself onto the bed.

"**OH, MY GOSH**, I'll be dead by then! What was I thinking?" I cry.

"Enough lollygagging," Dad says, pulling me up. "Time to go to work."

"Can I at least have my last meal?" I ask.

• • •

Once we finish breakfast, Dad and I put on our snow gear and bundle up tight. We exit through the garage and each pick up a shovel. Dad gets the heavy metal one with the wooden handle. He hands me a bright red one made of plastic.

"At least if I get buried in a snowdrift, you'll be able to find me," I say, waving my shovel.

Outside the world is calm and quiet. It's actually kind of nice.

"We'll start from the driveway and go to the front porch," Dad says. He starts shoveling a path. I follow next to him to make the path wider.

This isn't so bad, I think to myself.

We keep going for what feels like ages and my arms start to get tired.

"Are we there yet?" I moan.

"It's only halfway, Billy, come on. You can do it."

I huff and I puff behind my father until I've cleared my way to the porch. I am exhausted and fall backward onto a pile of snow.

"I'm just going to catch my breath for a couple of days right here," I say.

The cold air fills my lungs and hurts a little bit.

"Come on, champ. This is only round one. We gotta finish the driveway and head on over to Mr. Withers' house."

Dad pulls me up, and I look over at the window. Mom is standing there holding Ruby and waving hello. I wave back, pick up my shovel, and pretend I'm a Super Samurai on a mission.

Shoveling at super speed, I rush past my father and reach the sidewalk before him.

"Let's go, slowpoke," I yell.

He laughs, and we make it all the way up to Mr. Withers' house. After clearing out his driveway and sidewalk and the area around his door, Dad rings the bell.

Mr. Withers opens the door and smiles when he sees us. He is wearing a checkered robe, and his stringy white hair is sticking up in odd angles. He looks like a real mad scientist.

"Good morning, Marty," my father says.

"Well, lookee here, if it isn't the Burger boys! And they've shoveled my walkway. What a surprise!" replies Mr. Withers. "Please come in!"

My dad declines and says, "We really can't stay. We've got a lot more work ahead of us."

Mr. Withers reaches into his pocket and pulls out his wallet.

"At least let me pay you for your troubles!" he says.

He pulls out a wad of cash, and my eyes go wide. They turn into dollar signs.

CHA-CHING!

10
Cat-astrophe

"OOH, MONEY!" I shout. I reach out to grab it, but my father pulls me back by my jacket.

"Thank you for the generous offer, Mr. Withers. But we're not taking your money," Dad says sternly, eyeing me.

I hang my head.

"You see, it was Billy's idea that we volunteer our services and help our fellow neighbors," my dad continues as he puts his hand on my back.

I look at him, confused. He just smiles.

Then I look at Mr. Withers.

"Well, the young lad certainly takes after his father . . . *and* his grandfather," the old man says, looking down at me. "Your grandfather and I were friends and neighbors for over thirty years. That man was a model citizen. I'm glad you're following in his footsteps. He would be so proud!"

Wow, Mr. Withers thinks I'm a model citizen already. I must be doing something right, after all. Suddenly I feel a foot taller, as if I'm floating on air. It feels good to *do* good!

"We should get going, Dad," I say with new energy. "We have a lot more houses to shovel."

"May I suggest going to Mrs. Beakley's across the street?" Mr. Withers says. "Her daughter is away for the weekend. The woman's all alone in that house with the cat. She'll enjoy the company, I'm sure."

"You got it!" I announce. "Next stop, Mrs. Beakley's!"

As my dad and I head toward her house, we clear the sidewalk along the way. Dad scoops up a pile of snow and hurls it to the side. I follow behind him and do the same in the opposite direction. First Dad. Then me. We get a good rhythm going, like a locomotive. The warm breath coming out of my mouth and nose looks like steam.

"CHOO! CHOO!" I yell, startling my dad.

He smiles, shakes his head, and gets back to work.

I see a kid coming our way. He's dragging a blue Super Samurai sled behind him. It's Teddy!

"Hey, Teddy!" I yell, waving.

"Billy, I was just about to get you to go sledding!"

I look at him proudly and say that I am helping my fellow neighbors. I hold up my trusty shovel as if it were a sword.

"It is our Super Samurai duty to complete this mission," I add.

My friend smiles wide. "When you put it that way, Billy, I'm in! Let me get my dad, and we'll help too!"

And with that, Teddy turns around and runs back home.

"See, Billy?" Dad says. "Good deeds are contagious."

"Teddy knows that there's no business like snow business!" I smile and say.

We cross the street to Mrs. Beakley's house. Dad and I shovel out her walkway all the way to the front porch. Her yard is filled with little figurines and lawn ornaments that look like cats, but today they're all buried in the snow.

When we get close to the house, I notice a kitty banner hanging off the porch beam. It has a little kitten clinging to a tree branch with the words **HANG IN THERE** beneath it. I am watching it flap in the breeze when the door opens, and Mrs. Beakley invites us in.

"What nice young men you are! Come in and warm up. I have fresh-baked cookies and hot cocoa!"

"SAY WHAT?!" I shout. Cookies and cocoa sound good to me!

I drop the shovel and try to run in the snow, but it's almost up to my knees. Then I stop and remember my manners.

"Dad, can we go in?" I ask.

Dad says yes. "We could use a little more fuel," he adds.

Oh, man! I think. *This volunteer stuff certainly has its perks!*

Dad and I lean our shovels against the porch swing, stomp our boots on the welcome mat, and dust the snow off our jackets. Then we go inside.

The house is warm and toasty and smells like a cookie factory. I almost want to start chewing on the furniture, because everything smells like ooey-gooey chocolate chips. There is a drop of drool oozing down the side of my mouth. Those cookies are as good as mine!

All of a sudden I hear Mrs. Beakley scream.

"MITTENS, NO!"

I snap out of my snack-trance and look around.

"What happened?" Dad asks.

"My cat just ran out of the house!" Mrs. Beakley wails.

"SAY WHAT?!" I cry, looking back over my shoulder.

"Billy!" Dad yells. "You forgot to shut the door behind you!"

I rush to the door and watch in horror. *Drat, that cat!* I think.

Mittens is fast. She bounds down the freshly shoveled path. She's a furry brown bullet streaking against the white snow.

This is the second time in as many days that a furry little critter has turned my life upside down. I panic and decide that I should run after the cat before it's too late.

Dad sprints out the door first and leaps off the porch.

"Here we go again," I mutter and run out after him.

11

To the Rescue!

The snow crunches under our boots as we cut across the yard. If there's one thing I hate, it's ruining a smooth, snow-covered lawn. Unless I'm building a snow Samurai, of course.

"You go left, and I'll go right," Dad yells. "Try to bring that cat into the middle and grab her!"

I do as he says and run to the left. Mittens sees me, arches her back, and hisses. Then she sprints in the other direction.

My dad is waiting for her. I watch him corner the cat near a snowbank. He leans down to pick her up. But she hisses and swipes her claws at him.

"YOUCH!" he yelps.

"Do be careful!" warns Mrs. Beakley from the window. "She's a bit temperamental!"

"You don't say," Dad replies through gritted teeth.

He dives at mittens like a linebacker making a tackle. The cat leaps up and lands on my dad's back as he goes headfirst into the snowbank.

WHUMP!

I try not to laugh, but it's pretty funny. Dad's feet are kicking up and down. This is probably what I looked like when I was stuck under the sofa.

Dad pulls himself out. He's spitting snow and wiping his eyes.

Mittens watches Dad from a distance and licks the snow off her paws. Her tail is twitching back and forth. She seems to be enjoying herself.

Dad is on his feet again and has Mittens in his sights. "Not so fast, cat!" he shouts and races after her up the path back to Mrs. Beakley's house.

Suddenly I have a flashback to when I was chasing Franklin through the hallways at school. A lightbulb goes off inside my head.

"AHA!" I yell. "That's it!"

I rush over to the edge of the porch and try to climb onto the ledge. I pick up my right leg, but I can only get it a foot off the ground. I try the other leg and get the same result. I can barely move in my puffy snowsuit.

Okay, Billy, think! I say to myself.

I rush over to the other side of the patio and drag a snow-covered lawn chair toward the ledge. Out of the corner of my eye, I see Mrs. Beakley watching us from the window. She is clutching her necklace and biting her lip. She looks really worried.

Taking a deep breath, I step onto the lawn chair and then step onto the ledge. Normally, Dad would yell at me for pulling a stunt like this, but he's got his hands full.

I pull myself up and hold my arms out for balance. Then I reach for the cat banner on the flagpole.

Dad and Mittens are racing up the walkway. The cat is almost in the perfect position for my plan to work. Here goes nothing!

I quickly untie the rope holding the kitty banner in place. The rope comes loose as Mittens finally runs in front of the porch.

"It's curtains for you, fur ball!" I yell.

The wind blows the banner off the flagpole and it falls downward . . . right on top of Mittens!

WHUMP!

Just like how the stage curtain fell onto the archeologists yesterday! I think.

The crazed cat stops in her tracks, stunned for the moment.

"Smooth!" Dad calls out, still spitting snow from his mouth. He scoops up Mittens inside the banner and bundles her up so she's safe from the cold.

I hop down off the ledge and run after them. My heart is beating super fast from the excitement.

"Oh, thank you!" squeals Mrs. Beakley, taking Mittens into her arms. "You're my heroes!"

Did you hear that? I'm a **HERO!**

I blush when she gives us each a peck on the cheek.

12
Learning My Lessons

"That was some quick thinking, young man," Dad says. "I'm impressed."

"Me too!" says a voice.

I turn around to see Teddy.

"I saw you guys chasing the cat, and I ran right over here," he says. "It was like a replay from yesterday with the ferret. Guess you already had experience, huh?"

"Yeah, man," I say. "Don't remind me."

At that moment, Teddy's dad arrives with a number of other neighbors. They are all dressed in snowsuits and carrying shovels. One of them even has a high-tech snowblower.

"What's going on?" I ask.

"Check it out," Teddy says. He gestures with his arm at the group of people. "We got a whole squad to help!"

"SAY WHAT?!"

"I mentioned to my neighbor what you were up to, Billy," Teddy's dad says. "How you were helping those in need with your dad. Well, he told *his* neighbor, and she told *her* neighbor, and so on."

"Whoa," I say as it all starts to sink in. My good deeds were being used as an example by the people around me—just like back when Grandpa was alive.

"Thanks to you, we're helping each other and spending time together. And that makes us good neighbors," says Teddy's dad.

"I'm proud of you, son," Dad says, lightly squeezing my shoulder.

"That's because I'm Billy Burger, Model Citizen!" I say in my best superhero voice.

Teddy laughs and everyone else smiles.

Dad was right. Kindness really is contagious.

I feel kind of bad that I didn't want to do it in the first place, but doing good deeds really is worth it in the end. I just needed the right people to guide me.

From now on, I'll think of Grandma and Grandpa and what they would do in my place.

Mrs. Beakley claps her hands and says, "There's plenty of hot cocoa and cookies for everyone in the kitchen!"

The neighbors' faces light up with smiles. They cheer and clap and make their way up the path toward the house. I think of all those freshly baked cookies and make a dash for it.

"Not if I eat them first!" I shout. And I do, because they're delicious.

Maybe I shouldn't have, though, because now I feel sick.

But hey, I'm learning my lessons one at a time!

WHAT DO YOU THINK?

QUESTIONS TO THINK, TALK, AND WRITE ABOUT

1. Explain what it means to be a model citizen. Write about a model citizen from your school or community.

2. Choose one of the characters in the book and list five words or phrases to describe him or her. Then compare yourself to the character. How are you alike? In what ways are you different?

3. Imagine that Franklin's bite actually turned Billy into a mutant ferret man, and write a story about what happens to him next.

4. How does Mr. Karas feel after the curtain falls during the assembly? What details from the book tell you this?

5. When Billy helps his neighbors shovel, he says, "It feels good to do good!" Have you ever had that feeling? Write about a time you were helpful and how it made you feel.

Billy's Glossary

ancient artifacts—stuff that people used hundreds, or even thousands, of years ago; Mr. Karas says that ancient artifacts tell us how people lived and worked a long time ago

appetite—that feeling you get when you want something to eat; I have a very healthy and active appetite

archeologist—a scientist who studies past human life and all those ancient artifacts we talked about a few lines up

auditorium—this is the big room at my school where we go to listen to boring speakers, have concerts, and perform plays

chaos—when everyone is completely confused and shouting and running around, chances are that you are facing chaos

contagious—bad contagious means you catch something that makes you sick, but good contagious means people see something great happening and they can't help but join in

detective—when there is a crime, a detective is in charge of gathering clues and figuring out who did it

epic—super awesome; Probably more awesome than anything you've ever seen

expedition—a special trip that you make with a certain goal in mind, like discovering Samurai swords

fidgets—little movements that you might make when you are nervous, or if you're like me, bored in school

inspiration—an idea or feeling that you get from someone (like my grandfather) or something (like a TV show)

investigates—when my dad investigates things, he looks over them very closely, so he can solve the crimes

lollygagging—my dad's weird way of saying being slow and wasting time

mutant—when a person or animal is changed from normal form, probably by an alien or monster

rambunctious—a really long word for wild or unruly; When I occasionally forget to be a model citizen, I guess I might be a little, tiny bit rambunctious

severely—a grown-up way to say "really," as in, "Billy Burger, you could have severely hurt someone."

sorceress—a sorceress is basically a witch, but the word sounds a little cooler, right?

sorcery—using magic powers. I wish I had a little sorcery up my sleeve whenever I get caught by Principal Crank.

stealth—secret, sly movement; It takes real stealth to catch a free ferret

temperamental—judging from Mrs. Beakley's cat, Mittens, temperamental is another word for mean and nasty

tyrant—a terrible, cruel ruler . . . like Principal Crank

venom—poison that some animals make; They can pass their venom off to others by biting or stinging them . . . OUCH!

POOJA DHARAN

A REAL-LIFE MODEL CITIZEN

When Pooja Dharan visited India at age six, she saw many sad things, including children begging for food. She wanted to help but didn't know how.

Back in the United States, Pooja talked with her eight-year-old cousin, Dylan, who had seen the same things on his own trip to India. In 2004, they started an organization dedicated to helping people from around the world. Lil' MDGs has eight main goals, including ending poverty and fighting the spread of disease.

At first Pooja was in charge of Lil' MDGs' Facebook and Twitter feeds. But now she serves as CEO, leading many projects. Pooja has proven that young people can really make a difference.

She says, **"YOU ARE NEVER TOO YOUNG TO MAKE A DIFFERENCE.** If you have something that you would like to change about the world today, talk to a few friends about it and start a club. . . . The key is to find a few dedicated people like you, willing to create change, and you will definitely make a difference."

Lil' MDGs has found more than a few dedicated people; currently they have more than 24,000 volunteers!

To become involved,
visit www.lilmdgs.org
or email info@lilmdgs.org